But, with mien of lord or lady, perched
above my chamber door —
Perched upon a bust of Pallas just above my
chamber door —

   Perched, and sat, and nothing more.

In the deepest slumber — no! In delirium _ no! In a swoon _ no! In death _ no! even in the grave all is not lost.

Thy soul shall find itself alone
        'Mid dark thoughts of the gray tombstone —
Not one, of all the crowd, to pry
        Into thine hour of secrecy.

Pencil sketch of
Sarah Elmira Royster
by

Edgar A. Poe

"I've never encountered any writer who was so brilliantly able to transform his inner visions or hallucinations into universally loved fiction and poetry."

      – Vincent Price from the Introduction of *18 Best Stories by Edgar Allan Poe*, Dell Publishing 1965

# <u>Preface</u>

To say that Edgar Allan Poe has had an influence on me is an understatement, indeed.  My dark style of art (often Black & White) and my fascination with the paranormal had first developed when I read Poe's dark tales at an early age. I have been moved by the pure honesty that Poe shared as he poured his soul into his profound works, often writing in first-person as though he were recounting those harrowing experiences. From his words we each feel we understand him intimately— his fears, joys, passions, resentments, disappointments, and dreams— and I, therefore, endeavored to present this book in his own handwriting to give readers a greater, intimate understanding of the man.

Creating this book was an epic task, to say the least. The work was so complex and time-consuming that I felt as though I was caught in 'A Descent into the Maelstrom' of my own making. I had to create more than half-a-dozen alphabets with characters from Poe's writings that would flow easily enough into one another for a natural-looking ink flow.

I agonized over just the right selections, having already planned the overall length of the book. I know that many readers may be disappointed that I had not included other popular works such as *The Fall of the House of Usher, Ligeia,* or even *The Tell-Tale Heart.* Others may prefer that I had shown the lighter side of Poe with *The Balloon Hoax* or *The Sphinx.* An inclusion here of Poe's essays on

science and philosophy would have seemed ideal as
a showcase of his great intellect. Ultimately I
pressed to paint a portrait of Poe's deepest and most
personal fears by focusing mostly on his poems,
from which he was most telling of his truest self.
The three stories included here were selected
because of characters who stared Death keenly in
the eye, which certainly mirrored Poe's very personal awareness of inevitability. Other suitable
selections were considered, but were left out
because of various complexities that would be
difficult to reproduce believably in this type of
formatting. To compensate for some very notable
exclusions, I have restored several original
manuscripts in their entirety. I have carefully
painted out the blots and blemishes, while adding
fresh ink to give new life to these relics of Poe's
masterful penmanship.

Editing was a nightmare- there, I said it.
Computer crashes and change of word programs was
possibly less trying than my own stubborn OCD as I
fretted over each letter placement and size. Font
programs have the advantage of perfect letters, but
the disadvantage of line margins, so I had to choose
characters from Poe that didn't sweep too high nor
dip too low (favoring many of the characters in his
manuscript for Annabelle Lee, which appears in
this book in its original form). Reading old quill
writing is generally difficult, so I chose the best
lettering that would make for an easy and enjoyable
read, time and time again. In the end, the laborious
task has paid off as I am satisfied that fans of Poe
will cherish this book. The legacy of Edgar A. Poe

10

has endured the test of time as he still remains the
Master of the Macabre and one of America's- if not
the world's- most celebrated authors.

- Lee Allan

## Table of Contents



13

# <u>Introduction</u>

In describing Edgar Allan Poe (although I must note that he preferred to be called Edgar **A.** Poe in defiance of his estranged father-in-law, John Allan) I wanted to avoid tired cliches like "melancholy genius" or "tortured soul" and focus, instead, on the impressions of those that were most personally acquainted with him. In my research I came upon a very telling eulogy written by John Sartain titled, "Reminiscences of Edgar Allan Poe", which was published in March of 1889 in *Lippincott's Monthly Magazine*. Sartain published many of Poe's poems during his stint as editor of *Sartain's Union Magazine* from 1848 to 1852 and was the last friend to see Poe alive. Sartain's account of Poe's good intentions as well as his mental decline gives us a more complete and honest depiction of Poe in direct contrast to terse imputations from envious rivals. The original essay is too detailed and lengthy for inclusion in this Introduction, but a shorter and more succinct version appeared in *The Boston Evening Transcript* in 1893 that I will include herein with one break for clarification:

> "It was at the period of the transfer of Burton's Magazine to Graham that I first met Poe, already of much fame as a poet. He became one of my dearest friends. His memory I cherish and honor. He made many enemies, and many harsh things have been said about him, but I never once saw him drunk, and I believe that in everything he was perfectly hon-

est. To be sure, in his criticisms,
especially those in the Stylus, he used
'an iron pen,' and no doubt, as has been
said, 'sometimes mistook his vial of
prussic acid for his ink bottle. 'But I
believe he intended to be absolutely
fair in all that he wrote.

"As an instance of how far he was
above meaner motives, he actually
appointed as his literary executor a
clergyman whom he had once severely
criticised , not seeming to realize that
such a hauling over the coals could
never be forgotten. As a result, his
memory has suffered. That same clergyman, whose name is familiar to readers
of Poe literature was a notorious black-
mailer, and I myself had to pay him
money to prevent abusive notices of Sartain's Magazine.

The unscrupulous clergyman referenced by Sartain
was Rufus Griswold, a licensed Baptist, who began a
rivalry with Poe when the latter publically
criticized that Griswold's periodical, *The Poets
and Poetry of Society*, was "a most outrageous
humbug" and "unduly favored New England writers".
Griswold was later hired as editor of *Graham's
Magazine* with an even greater salary than its
former editor, Poe. Their rivalry became public
display when the two men vied for the company of a
young, talented poet named Frances "Fanny" Sargent
Locke, who had recently married Samuel Stillman
Osgood. Poe was married at this time to Virginia,

who was, by all accounts, suspicious of an affair between Fanny and her husband.  Trying to upstage one another from their various positions as editors gained both men reputations as being overly critical of freshman underlings, which earned Poe nicknames like "Tomahawk Man" and "Comanche of Literature" while his rival was called "The Griswold Hook".  Griswold would later write that Poe's death "will startle many, but few will be grieved by it". Sartain mentions the clergyman as being Poe's literary executor, which, according to Griswold, was an agreement by Poe in exchange for Griswold having published several of his poems, but there is no solid, legal grounds for this agreement. Rufus Griswold passed away on August 27, 1857 and, in an odd twist of irony, the only decorations found in his possession were portraits of himself, Fanny Osgood, and Edgar A. Poe.

"As for the charge that Poe was dishonest about his manuscripts, it has been said that he sold 'The Bells' to me thrice over. Indeed, he did sell the poem to me three times, but in an honest way.  It was accepted first as a poem of two stanzas.  Not being published for some time, Poe thrice added to it, and otherwise altered it.  Each time he deemed the poem worth more, and so did I, therefore paying him something extra in each case.

"The first instance of hallucination that I ever detected in Poe occurred

16

about a month before his tragic death. I was at work, in my shirt sleeves, in my office on Sansom street, when Poe burst in upon me excitedly, and exclaimed, 'I have come to you for refuge. 'I saw at a glance that he was suffering from some mental overstrain, and assured him of shelter. I then begged him to explain.

"'I was just on my way to New York on the train,' he said to me, 'when I heard whispering going on behind me. Owing to my marvellous power of hearing I was enabled to overhear what the conspirators were saying. Just imagine such a thing in this nineteenth century! They were plotting to murder me. I immediately left the train and hastened back here again. I must disguise myself in someway. I must shave off this mustache at once. Will you lend me a razor?'

"Afraid to trust him with it, I told him I hadn't any, but that I could remove his moustache [*sic*] with the scissors. Taking him to the rear of the office I sheared away until he was absolutely barefaced. This satisfied him somewhat and I managed to calm him. That very evening, however, he prepared to leave the house. 'Where are you going?' I asked. 'To the Schuylkill,' he replied. 'Then I am going along with you,' I declared. He did not object, and

together we walked to Chestnut street
and took a 'bus.

"A steep flight of steps used to
lead up from the Schuylkill then, and
ascending these we sat on a bench over-
looking the stream.  The night was
black , without a star, and I felt somewhat nervous alone with Poe in the condition he was in.  Going up in the 'bus he
said to me, 'After my death see that my
mother (Mrs. Clemm) gets that portrait of
me from Osgood.'

"Now he began to talk the wildest non-
sense, in the weird, dramatic style of
his tales. He said he had been thrown
into Moyamensing Prison for forging a
check, and while there a white female
form had appeared on the battlements
and addressed him in whispers.

"'If I had not heard what she said,' he
declared, 'it would have been the end of
me. But, owing to my marvellous hearing,
I lost not a single word. Then another
figure appeared and invited me to walk
with him around the battlements.  He
conducted me to a caldron of liquid, and
asked me if I wished a drink. I refused,
for that was a trap. Do you know what
would have happened if I had accepted?
They would have lifted me over the
caldron, and placed me in the liquid up

18

to my lips, like Tantalus, and gone away
and left me there.'

"By and by I suggested that we
descend again and Poe assented. All the
way down the steep steps I trembled lest
he should remember his resolve of suic-
ide, but I kept his mind from it and got
him back safely. Three days after he went
out again and returned in the same mood.
'I lay on the earth with my nose in the
grass,' he said then, 'and the smell
revived me. I began at once to realize
the falsity of my hallucinations.'

"A month later he left Washington
to meet his bride. A storm deterred him
from crossing at Havre de Grace and he
returned to Baltimore. Behind him, in
the car, even as in his hallucination,
sat a number of suspicious-looking persons. When Poe passed down one of the
streets they followed at his heels. Poe
was well dressed and undoubtedly had
money in his Pockets. The next morning
he was found in a vacant lot, nearly
dead. He was clad in shabby clothes and
had evidently been drugged. When,
later, beseeched at the hospital to
drink a toddy, he put up his hand and
waved it off — and thus he died."

The exact cause(s) of Poe's death has remained
a subject of much debate, but Sartain's own account

of those final moments gives some credence to recent theories that may finally solve the mystery:

Sartain recounted the "suspicious-looking persons" responsible for his friend's paranoia as they "followed at his heels", which had caused Poe an urgent need to disguise himself by removing his mustache. Sartain made mention that the "shabby clothes" found on Poe on that tragic morning were distinctly different from those "well dressed" clothes the day prior. "Evidently been drugged", as Sartain described, gives yet another validation to a theory that Poe was the victim of "cooping".

Poe was found in delirium on Election Day near Gunner's Hall, which was a polling station, so a theory that has reached a popular consensus is that he was a victim of cooping, which was a common method of voter fraud in the 19th Century. Victims of this practice were kidnapped, drugged or forced to drink alcohol, and disguised repeatedly in order to cast multiple votes. On the final night of his life while in hospital care, Poe incessantly called out the name, "Reynolds", possibly a refer- ence to a campaign poll judge in the Fourth Ward named Henry R. Reynolds- an interesting connection to a Reynolds that might validate the cooping theory, but it is important to note that Poe had once edited a piece on whale fishing written by Jeremiah N. Reynolds- the same name that appears on a bankruptcy petition written by Poe in 1847.

Cooping may explain some of the mystery surrounding Poe's death, but not all of it. Although forcing a victim of cooping to drink alcohol was common, Poe's state of apparent delirium is almost certainly not the cause of drunkeness. Excessive drinking in his younger years had eventually made Poe so sensitive to alcohol that a single glass of wine would make him violently ill for days. Sartain alludes to Poe's aversion to alcohol in the preceding article in which he states he "never once saw him drunk" and when Poe was offered a toddy in the hospital per medical practice, Sartain wrote that Poe "put up his hand and waved it off".  Pathology experts have since studied the attending physician's notes regarding Poe's hospital stay and concluded that the delirium must have been the result of rabies.

Rabies was earlier called hydrophobia in reference to the afflicted's inability to swallow fluids due to painful throat spasms, which may give yet another explanation for Poe's refusal to drink the offered toddy. Poe showed other key symptoms of rabies, as well, as he perspired profusely and had fits of hallucinations. There is no account of Poe ever being bitten by an animal, but 25% of rabies patients can't remember being bitten. Since rabies can sometimes take up to a year to develop symptoms after a bite, one can look to Poe's past practice of feeding stray cats as a possible bite incident- an act of kindness that perhaps lead to a tragic ending.

# Alone.

From childhood's hour I have not been
As others were — I have not seen
As others saw — I could not bring
My passions from a common spring —
From the same source I have not taken
My sorrow — I could not awaken
My heart to joy at the same tone —
Then — in my childhood — in the dawn
Of a most stormy life — was drawn
From ev'ry depth of good and ill
The mystery which binds me still —
From the torrent, or the fountain —
From the red cliff of the mountain —
From the sun that 'round me roll'd
In its autumn tint of gold —
From the lightning in the sky
As it pass'd me flying by —
From the thunder, and the storm —
And the cloud that took the form
(When the rest of Heaven was blue)
Of a demon in my view —

# The Spirits of the Dead.

Thy soul shall find itself alone
   'Mid dark thoughts of the gray tombstone —
Not one, of all the crowd, to pry
   Into thine hour of secrecy.


Be silent in that solitude,
   Which is not loneliness — for then
The spirits of the dead who stood
   In life before thee are again
In death around thee — and their will
   Shall overshadow thee: be still.


The night, tho' clear, shall frown —
   And the stars shall look not down
From their high thrones in the heaven,
   With light like Hope to mortals given —
But their red orbs, without beam,
   To thy weariness shall seem
As a burning and a fever
   Which would cling to thee for ever.

Now are thoughts thou shalt not banish,
  Now are visions ne'er to vanish;
From thy spirit shall they pass
  No more — like dew-drop from the grass.
The breeze — the breath of God — is still —
  And the mist upon the hill,
Shadowy — shadowy — yet unbroken,
  Is a symbol and a token —
How it hangs upon the trees,
  A mystery of mysteries!

# A Descent into the Maelström

> The ways of God in Nature, as in
> Providence, are not as our ways;
> nor are the models that we frame
> any way commensurate to the vast-
> ness, profundity, and unsearchable-
> ness of His works, which have a
> depth in them greater than the well
> of Democritus.
>
> — Joseph Glanville.

We had now reached the summit of the loftiest crag. For some minutes the old man seemed too much exhausted to speak.

"Not long ago," said he at length, "and I could have guided you on this route as well as the youngest of my sons; but, about three years past, there happened to me an event such as never happened to mortal man — or at least such as no man ever survived to tell of — and the six hours of deadly terror which I then endured have broken me up body and soul. You suppose me a very old man — but I am not. It took less than a single day to change these hairs from a jetty black to white, to weaken my limbs, and to unstring my nerves, so that I tremble at the least exertion, and am frightened at a shadow. Do you know I can scarcely look over this little cliff without getting giddy?"

The "little cliff," upon whose edge he had so carelessly thrown himself down to rest that the weightier portion of his body hung over it, while he was only kept from falling by the tenure of his elbow on its extreme and slippery edge — this "little cliff" arose, a sheer unobstructed precipice of black shining rock, some fifteen or sixteen hundred feet from the world of crags beneath us. Nothing would have tempted me to within half a dozen yards of its brink. In truth so deeply was I excited by the perilous position of my companion, that I fell at full length upon the ground, clung to the shrubs around me, and dared not even glance upward at the sky — while I struggled in vain to divest myself of the idea that the very foundations of the mountain were in danger from the fury of the winds. It was long before I could reason myself into sufficient courage to sit up and look out into the distance.

"You must get over these fancies," said the guide, "for I have brought you here that you might have the best possible view of the scene of that event I mentioned _ and to tell you the whole story with the spot just under your eye."

"We are now," he continued, in that particularizing manner which distinguished him — "we are now close upon the Norwegian coast _ in the sixty-eighth degree of latitude — in the great province of Nordland — and in the dreary district of Lofoden. The mountain upon whose top we sit is Helseggen, the Cloudy. Now raise yourself up a little higher — hold on to the grass if you feel giddy — so _ and look out, beyond the belt of vapor beneath us, into the sea."

I looked dizzily, and beheld a wide expanse of ocean, whose waters wore so inky a

hue as to bring at once to my mind the Nubian
geographer's account of the Mare Tenebrarum. A
panorama more deplorably desolate no human
imagination can conceive. To the right and left,
as far as the eye could reach, there lay outstretched, like ramparts of the world, lines of
horridly black and beetling cliff, whose character of gloom was but the more forcibly illu-
strated by the surf which reared high up
against its white and ghastly crest, howling
and shrieking forever. Just opposite the pro-
montory upon whose apex we were placed, and at
a distance of some five or six miles out at sea,
there was visible a small, bleak-looking island;
or, more properly, its position was discernible
through the wilderness of surge in which it was
enveloped. About two miles nearer the land,
arose another of smaller size, hideously craggy
and barren, and encompassed at various
intervals by a cluster of dark rocks.

The appearance of the ocean, in the space
between the more distant island and the shore,
had something very unusual about it. Although,

29

at the time, so strong a gale was blowing landward that a brig in the remote offing lay to under a double-reefed trysail, and constantly plunged her whole hull out of sight, still there was here nothing like a regular swell, but only a short, quick, angry cross dashing of water in every direction — as well in the teeth of the wind as otherwise. Of foam there was little except in the immediate vicinity of the rocks.

" The island in the distance," resumed the old man, " is called by the Norwegians Vurrgh. The one midway is Moskoe. That a mile to the northward is Ambaaren. Yonder are Islesen, Hotholm, Keildhelm, Suarven, and Buckholm. Farther off — between Moskoe and Vurrgh — are Otterholm, Flimen, Sand-flesen, and Stockholm. These are the true names of the places — but why it has been thought necessary to name them at all, is more than either you or I can understand. Do you hear anything? Do you see any change in the water? "

We had now been about ten minutes upon the top of Helseggen, to which we had ascended from the interior of Lofoden, so that we had caught no glimpse of the sea until it had burst upon us from the summit. As the old man spoke, I became aware of a loud and gradually increasing sound, like the moaning of a vast herd of buffaloes upon an American prairie; and at the same moment I perceived that what seamen term the chopping character of the ocean beneath us, was rapidly changing into a current which set to the eastward. Even while I gazed, this current acquired a monstrous velocity. Each moment added to its speed — to its headlong impetuosity. In five minutes the whole sea, as far as Vurrgh, was lashed into ungovernable fury; but it was between Moskoe and the coast that the main uproar held its sway. Here the vast bed of the waters, seamed and scarred into a thousand conflicting chan-nels, burst suddenly into phrensied convul-sion — heaving, boiling, hissing — gyrating in gigantic and innumerable vortices, and all whirling and plunging on to the eastward

31

with a rapidity which water never elsewhere
assumes except in precipitous descents.

In a few minutes more, there came over
the scene another radical alteration. The
general surface grew somewhat more smooth, and
the whirlpools, one by one, disappeared, while
prodigious streaks of foam became apparent
where none had been seen before. These
streaks, at length, spreading out to a great
distance, and entering into combination, took
unto themselves the gyratory motion of the
subsided vortices, and seemed to form the germ
of another more vast. Suddenly — very
suddenly — this assumed a distinct and definite existence, in a circle of more than a mile
in diameter. The edge of the whirl was represented by a broad belt of gleaming spray; but
no particle of this slipped into the mouth of the
terrific funnel, whose interior, as far as the
eye could fathom it, was a smooth, shining,
and jet-black wall of water, inclined to the
horizon at an angle of some forty-five degrees,
speeding dizzily round and round with a
swaying and sweltering motion, and sending

32

forth to the winds an appalling voice, half shriek, half roar, such as not even the mighty cataract of Niagara ever lifts up in its agony to Heaven.

The mountain trembled to its very base, and the rock rocked. I threw myself upon my face, and clung to the scant herbage in an excess of nervous agitation.

"This," said I at length, to the old man — "this can be nothing else than the great whirl-pool of the Maelström."

"So it is sometimes termed," said he. "We Norwegians call it the Moskoe-ström, from the island of Moskoe in the midway."

The ordinary accounts of this vortex had by no means prepared me for what I saw. That of Jonas Ramus, which is perhaps the most cir-cumstantial of any, cannot impart the faint-est conception either of the magnificence, or of the horror of the scene — or of the wild bewild-ering sense of the novel which confounds the beholder. I am not sure from what point of

33

view the writer in question surveyed it, nor at what time; but it could neither have been from the summit of Helseggen, nor during a storm. There are some passages of his description, nevertheless, which may be quoted for their details, although their effect is exceedingly feeble in conveying an impression of the spectacle.

"Between Lofoden and Moskoe," he says, " the depth of the water is between thirty-six and forty fathoms; but on the other side, toward Ver (Vurrgh) this depth decreases so as not to afford a convenient passage for a vessel, without the risk of splitting on the rocks, which happens even in the calmest weather. When it is flood, the stream runs up the country between Lofoden and Moskoe with a boisterous rapidity; but the roar of its impetuous ebb to the sea is scarce equalled by the loudest and most dreadful cataracts; the noise being heard several leagues off, and the vortices or pits are of such an extent and depth, that if a ship comes within its attraction, it is inevitably absorbed and carried down to the bottom, and there beat to pieces against the rocks; and when the water relaxes, the fragments thereof are thrown up again. But these intervals of tranquility are only at the turn of the ebb and flood, and in calm weather, and last but a quarter of an hour, its violence gradually returning. When the stream is most boisterous, and its fury heightened by a storm, it is dangerous to come within a Norway mile of it. Boats, yachts, and ships have been carried away by not guarding against it before they were within its reach. It likewise happens frequently, that whales come too near the stream, and are overpowered by its violence; and then it is impossible to describe their howlings and bellowings in their fruitless struggles to disengage themselves. A bear once, attempting to swim from Lofoden to Moskoe, was caught by the stream and borne down, while he roared terribly, so as to be heard on shore. Large stocks of firs and pine trees, after being absorbed by the current, rise again broken and torn to such a degree as if bristles grew upon them. This plainly shows the bottom to consist of craggy rocks, among which they are whirled to and fro. This stream is regulated by the flux and reflux of the sea — it being constantly high and low water every six hours. In the year 1645 , early in the morning of Sexagesima Sunday, it raged with such noise and impetuosity that the very stones of the houses on the coast fell to the ground."

In regard to the depth of the water, I could not see how this could have been ascertained at all in the immediate vicinity of the vortex. The "forty fathoms" must have reference only to portions of the channel close upon the shore either of Moskoe or Lofoden. The depth in the centre of the Moskoe-ström must be immeasurably greater; and no better proof of this fact is necessary than can be obtained from even the sidelong glance into the abyss of the whirl which may be had from the highest crag of Helseggen. Looking down from this pinnacle upon the howling Phlegethon below, I could not help smiling at the simplicity with which the honest Jonas Ramus records, as a matter difficult of belief, the anecdotes of the whales and the bears; for it appeared to me, in fact, a self-evident thing, that the largest ship of the line in existence, coming within the influence of that deadly attraction, could resist it as little as a feather the hurricane, and must disappear bodily and at once.

The attempts to account for the phenomenon — some of which, I remember, seemed to me sufficiently plausible in perusal — now wore a very different and unsatisfactory aspect. The idea generally received is that this, as well as three smaller vortices among the Ferroe islands, "have no other cause than the collision of waves rising and falling, at flux and reflux, against a ridge of rocks and shelves, which confines the water so that it precipitates itself like a cataract; and thus the higher the flood rises, the deeper must the fall be, and the natural result of all is a whirlpool or vortex, the prodigious suction of which is sufficiently known by lesser experiments." — These are the words of the Encyclopædia Britannica. Kircher and others imagine that in the centre of the channel of the Maelström is an abyss penetrating the globe, and issuing in some very remote part — the Gulf of Bothnia being somewhat decidedly named in one instance. This opinion, idle in itself, was the one to which, as I gazed, my imagination most readily assented; and, mentioning it to the guide, I was rather surprised to hear him say that, although it was the view almost universally entertained of the subject by the Norwegians, it nevertheless was not his own. As to the former notion he confessed his inability to comprehend it; and here I agreed with him — for, however conclusive on paper, it becomes altogether unintelligible, and even absurd, amid the thunder of the abyss.

"You have had a good look at the whirl now," said the old man, "and if you will creep round this crag, so as to get in its lee, and deaden the roar of the water, I will tell you a story that will convince you I ought to know something of the Moskoe-ström."

I placed myself as desired, and he proceeded.

"Myself and my two brothers once owned a schooner-rigged smack of about seventy tons burthen, with which we were in the habit of fishing among the islands beyond Moskoe, nearly to Vurrgh. In all violent eddies at sea there is good fishing, at proper opportunities, if one has only the courage to attempt it; but among the whole of the Lofoden coastmen, we three were the only ones who made a regular business of going out to the islands, as I tell you. The usual grounds are a great way lower down to the southward. There fish can be got at all hours, without much risk, and therefore these places are preferred. The choice spots over here among the rocks, however, not only yield the finest variety, but in far greater abundance; so that we often got in a single day, what the more timid of the craft could not scrape together in a week. In fact, we made it a matter of desperate speculation — the risk of life standing instead of labor, and courage answering for capital.

"We kept the smack in a cove about five miles higher up the coast than this; and it was our practice, in fine weather, to take advantage of the fifteen minutes' slack to push across the main channel of the Moskoe-ström, far above the pool, and then drop down upon anchorage somewhere near Otterholm, or Sand-flesen, where the eddies are not so violent as elsewhere. Here we used to remain until nearly time for slack-water again, when we weighed and made for home. We never set out upon this expedition without a steady side wind for going and coming — one that we felt sure would not fail us before our return — and we seldom made a miscalculation upon this point. Twice, during six years, we were forced to stay all night at anchor on account of a dead calm, which is a rare thing indeed just about here; and once we had to remain on the grounds nearly a week, starving to death, owing to a gale which blew up shortly after our arrival, and made the channel too boisterous to be thought of. Upon this occasion we should have been driven out to sea in spite of everything, (for the whirlpools threw us round and round so violently, that, at length, we fouled our

40

anchor and dragged it) if it had not been that we drifted into one of the innumerable cross currents — here to-day and gone to-morrow — which drove us under the lee of Flimen, where, by good luck, we brought up.

"I could not tell you the twentieth part of the difficulties we encountered 'on the ground' — it is a bad spot to be in, even in good weather — but we made shift always to run the gauntlet of the Moskoe-ström itself without accident; although at times my heart has been in my mouth when we happened to be a minute or so behind or before the slack. The wind sometimes was not as strong as we thought it at starting, and then we made rather less way than we could wish, while the current rendered the smack unmanageable. My eldest brother had a son eighteen years old, and I had two stout boys of my own. These would have been of great assistance at such times, in using the sweeps, as well as afterward in fishing — but, somehow, although we ran the risk ourselves, we had not the heart to let the young ones get into the danger — for, after all is said and

41

done, it was a horrible danger, and that is the truth.

"It is now within a few days of three years since what I am going to tell you occurred. It was on the tenth day of July, 18—, a day which the people of this part of the world will never forget — for it was one in which blew the most terrible hurricane that ever came out of the heavens. And yet all the morning, and indeed until late in the afternoon, there was a gentle and steady breeze from the south-west, while the sun shone brightly, so that the oldest seaman among us could not have foreseen what was to follow.

"The three of us — my two brothers and myself — had crossed over to the islands about two o'clock P.M., and had soon nearly loaded the smack with fine fish, which, we all remarked, were more plenty that day than we had ever known them. It was just seven, by my watch, when we weighed and started for home, so as to make the worst of the Ström at slack water, which we knew would be at eight.

42

" We set out with a fresh wind on our starboard quarter, and for some time spanked along at a great rate, never dreaming of danger, for indeed we saw not the slightest reason to apprehend it. All at once we were taken aback by a breeze from over Helseggen. This was most unusual — something that had never happened to us before — and I began to feel a little uneasy, without exactly knowing why. We put the boat on the wind, but could make no headway at all for the eddies, and I was upon the point of proposing to return to the anchorage, when, looking astern, we saw the whole horizon covered with a singular copper-colored cloud that rose with the most amazing velocity.

"In the meantime the breeze that had headed us off fell away, and we were dead becalmed, drifting about in every direction. This state of things, however, did not last long enough to give us time to think about it. In less than a minute the storm was upon us — in less than two the sky was entirely over-cast — and what with this and the driving

43

spray, it became suddenly so dark that we could not see each other in the smack.

"Such a hurricane as then blew it is folly to attempt describing. The oldest seaman in Norway never experienced any thing like it. We had let our sails go by the run before it cleverly took us; but, at the first puff, both our masts went by the board as if they had been sawed off — the mainmast taking with it my youngest brother, who had lashed himself to it for safety.

" Our boat was the lightest feather of a thing that ever sat upon water. It had a complete flush deck, with only a small hatch near the bow, and this hatch it had always been our custom to batten down when about to cross the Ström, by way of precaution against the chopping seas. But for this circumstance we should have foundered at once — for we lay entirely buried for some moments. How my elder brother escaped destruction I cannot say, for I never had an opportunity of ascertaining. For my part, as soon as I had let the

44

foresail run, I threw myself flat on deck, with my feet against the narrow gunwale of the bow, and with my hands grasping a ring-bolt near the foot of the fore-mast. It was mere instinct that prompted me to do this — which was undoubtedly the very best thing I could have done — for I was too much flurried to think.

"For some moments we were completely deluged, as I say, and all this time I held my breath, and clung to the bolt. When I could stand it no longer I raised myself upon my knees, still keeping hold with my hands, and thus got my head clear. Presently our little boat gave herself a shake, just as a dog does in coming out of the water, and thus rid herself, in some measure, of the seas. I was now trying to get the better of the stupor that had come over me, and to collect my senses so as to see what was to be done, when I felt somebody grasp my arm. It was my elder brother, and my heart leaped for joy, for I had made sure that he was overboard — but the next moment

45

all this joy was turned into horror — for he put his mouth close to my ear, and screamed out the word "Moskoe-ström!"

"No one ever will know what my feelings were at that moment. I shook from head to foot as if I had had the most violent fit of the ague. I knew what he meant by that one word well enough — I knew what he wished to make me understand. With the wind that now drove us on, we were bound for the whirl of the Ström, and nothing could save us!

"You perceive that in crossing the Ström channel, we always went a long way up above the whirl, even in the calmest weather, and then had to wait and watch carefully for the slack — but now we were driving right upon the pool itself, and in such a hurricane as this! "To be sure," I thought, "we shall get there just about the slack — there is some little hope in that" — but in the next moment I cursed myself for being so great a fool as to dream of hope at all. I knew very well that we were doomed, had we been ten times a ninety-gun ship.

"By this time the first fury of the tempest had spent itself, or perhaps we did not feel it so much, as we scudded before it, but at all events the seas, which at first had been kept down by the wind, and lay flat and frothing, now got up into absolute mountains. A singular change, too, had come over the heavens. Around in every direction it was still as black as pitch, but nearly overhead there burst out, all at once, a circular rift of clear sky — as clear as I ever saw — and of a deep bright blue — and through it there blazed forth the full moon with a lustre that I never before knew her to wear. She lit up every thing about us with the greatest distinctness — but, oh God, what a scene it was to light up!

"I now made one or two attempts to speak to my brother — but, in some manner which I could not understand, the din had so increased that I could not make him hear a single word, although I screamed at the top of my voice in his ear. Presently he shook his head, looking as pale as death, and held up one of his fingers, as if to say "listen!"

47

"At first I could not make out what he meant — but soon a hideous thought flashed upon me. I dragged my watch from its fob. It was not going. I glanced at its face by the moon-light, and then burst into tears as I flung it far away into the ocean. It had run down at seven o'clock. We were behind the time of the slack, and the whirl of the Ström was in full fury!

"When a boat is well built, properly trimmed and not deep laden, the waves in a strong gale, when she is going large, seem always to slip from beneath her — which appears very strange to a landsman — and this is what is called riding, in sea phrase.

"Well, so far we had ridden the swells very cleverly; but presently a gigantic sea happened to take us right under the counter, and bore us with it as it rose — up — up — up — as if into the sky. I would not have believed that any wave could rise so high. And then down we came with a sweep, a slide, and a plunge, that made me feel sick and dizzy, as

48

if I was falling from some lofty mountaintop in a dream. But while we were up I had thrown a quick glance around — and that one glance was all sufficient. I saw our exact position in an instant. The Moskoe-Ström whirlpool was about a quarter of a mile dead ahead — but no more like the every-day Moskoe-Ström, than the whirl as you now see it is like a mill-race. If I had not known where we were, and what we had to expect, I should not have recognised the place at all. As it was, I involuntarily closed my eyes in horror. The lids clenched themselves together as if in a spasm.

"It could not have been more than two minutes afterward until we suddenly felt the waves subside, and were enveloped in foam. The boat made a sharp half turn to larboard, and then shot off in its new direction like a thunderbolt. At the same moment the roaring noise of the water was completely drowned in a kind of shrill shriek — such a sound as you might imagine given out by the waste-pipes of many thousand steam-vessels, letting off their steam all together. We were now in the belt of surf that always surrounds the whirl; and I thought, of course, that another moment would plunge us into the abyss — down which we could only see indistinctly on account of the amazing velocity with which we were borne along. The boat did not seem to sink into the water at all, but to skim like an air-bubble upon the surface of the surge. Her starboard side was next the whirl, and on the larboard arose the world of ocean we had left. It stood like a huge writhing wall between us and the horizon.

"It may appear strange, but now, when we were in the very jaws of the gulf, I felt more composed than when we were only approaching it. Having made up my mind to hope no more, I got rid of a great deal of that terror which unmanned me at first. I suppose it was despair that strung my nerves.

"It may look like boasting — but what I tell you is truth — I began to reflect how magnificent a thing it was to die in such a manner, and how foolish it was in me to think of so paltry a consideration as my own individual life, in view of so wonderful a manifestation of God's power. I do believe that I blushed with shame when this idea crossed my mind. After a little while I became possessed with the keenest curiosity about the whirl itself. I positively felt a wish to explore its depths, even at the sacrifice I was going to make; and my principal grief was that I should never be able to tell my old companions on shore about the mysteries I should see. These, no doubt, were singular fancies to occupy a man's mind in such extremity — and I have often thought since, that the revolutions of the boat around the pool might have rendered me a little light-headed.

"There was another circumstance which tended to restore my self-possession; and this was the cessation of the wind, which could not reach us in our present situation — for, as you saw yourself, the belt of surf is considerably lower than the general bed of the ocean, and this latter now towered above us, a high, black, mountainous ridge. If you have never

51

been at sea in a heavy gale, you can form no idea of the confusion of mind occasioned by the wind and spray together. They blind, deafen, and strangle you, and take away all power of action or reflection. But we were now, in a great measure, rid of these annoyances — just us death-condemned felons in prison are allowed petty indulgences, forbidden them while their doom is yet uncertain.

" How often we made the circuit of the belt it is impossible to say. We careered round and round for perhaps an hour, flying rather than floating, getting gradually more and more into the middle of the surge, and then nearer and nearer to its horrible inner edge. All this time I had never let go of the ring-bolt. My brother was at the stern, holding on to a small empty water-cask which had been securely lashed under the coop of the counter, and was the only thing on deck that had not been swept overboard when the gale first took us. As we approached the brink of the pit he let go his hold upon this, and made for the ring, from which, in the agony of his terror, he endeavored to force my hands, as it was not large enough to afford us both a secure grasp. I never felt deeper grief than when I saw him attempt this act — although I knew he was a madman when he did it — a raving maniac through sheer fright. I did not care, however, to contest the point with him. I knew it could make no difference whether either of us held on at all; so I let him have the bolt, and went astern to the cask. This there was no great difficulty in doing; for the smack flew round steadily enough, and upon an even keel — only swaying to and fro, with the immense sweeps and swelters of the whirl. Scarcely had I secured myself in my new position, when we gave a wild lurch to starboard, and rushed headlong into the abyss. I muttered a hurried prayer to God, and thought all was over.

"As I felt the sickening sweep of the descent, I had instinctively tightened my hold upon the barrel, and closed my eyes. For some seconds I dared not open them — while I expected instant destruction, and wondered that I was not already in my death-struggles with the water. But moment after moment elapsed. I still lived. The sense of falling had ceased; and the motion of the vessel seemed much as it had been before, while in the belt of foam, with the exception that she now lay more along. I took courage, and looked once again upon the scene.

"Never shall I forget the sensations of awe, horror, and admiration with which I gazed about me. The boat appeared to be hanging, as if by magic, midway down, upon the interior surface of a funnel vast in circumference, prodigious in depth, and whose perfectly smooth sides might have been mistaken for ebony, but for the bewildering rapidity with which they spun around, and for the gleaming and ghastly radiance they shot forth, as the rays of the full moon, from that circular rift amid the clouds which I have already described, streamed in a flood of golden glory along the black walls, and far away down into the inmost recesses of the abyss.

"At first I was too much confused to observe anything accurately. The general burst of terrific grandeur was all that I beheld. When I recovered myself a little, however, my gaze fell instinctively downward. In this direction I was able to obtain an unobstructed view, from the manner in which the smack hung on the inclined surface of the pool. She was quite upon an even keel — that is to say, her deck lay in a plane parallel with that of the water — but this latter sloped at an angle of more than forty-five degrees, so that we seemed to be lying upon our beam-ends. I could not help observing, nevertheless, that I had scarcely more difficulty in maintaining my hold and footing in this situation, than if we had been upon a dead level; and this, I suppose, was owing to the speed at which we revolved.

"The rays of the moon seemed to search the very bottom of the profound gulf; but still I could make out nothing distinctly, on account of

55

a thick mist in which everything there was enveloped, and over which there hung a magnificent rainbow, like that narrow and tottering bridge which Mussulmen say is the only pathway between Time and Eternity. This mist, or spray, was no doubt occasioned by the clashing of the great walls of the funnel, as they all met together at the bottom — but the yell that went up to the Heavens from out of that mist, I dare not attempt to describe.

"Our first slide into the abyss itself, from the belt of foam above, had carried us a great distance down the slope; but our farther descent was by no means proportionate. Round and round we swept — not with any uniform movement — but in dizzying swings and jerks, that sent us sometimes only a few hundred yards — sometimes nearly the complete circuit of the whirl. Our progress downward, at each revolution, was slow, but very perceptible.

"Looking about me upon the wide waste of liquid ebony on which we were thus borne, I perceived that our boat was not the only object

56

in the embrace of the whirl. Both above and below us were visible fragments of vessels, large masses of building timber and trunks of trees, with many smaller articles, such as pieces of house furniture, broken boxes, barrels and staves. I have already described the unnatural curiosity which had taken the place of my original terrors. It appeared to grow upon me as I drew nearer and nearer to my dreadful doom. I now began to watch, with a strange interest, the numerous things that floated in our company. I must have been delirious — for I even sought amusement in speculating upon the relative velocities of their several descents toward the foam below. "This fir tree," I found myself at one time saying, "will certainly be the next thing that takes the awful plunge and disappears;" — and then I was disappointed to find that the wreck of a Dutch merchant ship overtook it and went down before. At length, after making several guesses of this nature, and being deceived in all — this fact — the fact of my invariable miscalculation — set me upon a train of reflec-

tion that made my limbs again tremble, and my
heart beat heavily once more.

"It was not a new terror that thus affected
me, but the dawn of a more exciting hope. This
hope arose partly from memory, and partly
from present observation. I called to mind the
great variety of buoyant matter that strewed the
coast of Lofoden, having been absorbed and then
thrown forth by the Moskoe-ström. By far the
greater number of the articles were shattered in
the most extraordinary way — so chafed and
roughened as to have the appearance of being
stuck full of splinters — but then I distinctly
recollected that there were some of them which
were not disfigured at all. Now I could not
account for this difference except by supposing
that the roughened fragments were the only ones
which had been completely absorbed — that the
others had entered the whirl at so late a period
of the tide, or, for some reason, had descended
so slowly after entering, that they did not
reach the bottom before the turn of the flood
came, or of the ebb, as the case might be. I

conceived it possible, in either instance, that they might thus be whirled up again to the level of the ocean, without undergoing the fate of those which had been drawn in more early, or absorbed more rapidly. I made, also, three important observations. The first was, that, as a general rule, the larger the bodies were, the more rapid their descent — the second, that, between two masses of equal extent, the one spherical, and the other of any other shape, the superiority in speed of descent was with the sphere — the third, that, between two masses of equal size, the one cylindrical, and the other of any other shape, the cylinder was absorbed the more slowly. Since my escape, I have had several conversations on this subject with an old school-master of the district; and it was from him that I learned the use of the words "cylinder" and "sphere." He explained to me — although I have forgotten the explanation — how what I observed was, in fact, the natural cons- equence of the forms of the floating fragments — and showed me how it happened that a cylinder, swimming in a vortex, offered more resistance

59

to its suction, and was drawn in with greater difficulty than an equally bulky body, of any form whatever.

"There was one startling circumstance which went a great way in enforcing these observations, and rendering me anxious to turn them to account, and this was that, at every revolution, we passed something like a barrel, or else the yard or the mast of a vessel, while many of these things, which had been on our level when I first opened my eyes upon the wonders of the whirlpool, were now high up above us, and seemed to have moved but little from their original station.

"I no longer hesitated what to do. I resolved to lash myself securely to the water cask upon which I now held, to cut it loose from the counter, and to throw myself with it into the water. I attracted my brother's attention by signs, pointed to the floating barrels that came near us, and did everything in my power to make him understand what I was about to do. I thought at length that he comprehended my design — but, whether this was the case or not, he shook his head despairingly, and refused to move from his station by the ring-bolt. It was impossible to reach him; the emergency admitted of no delay; and so, with a bitter struggle, I resigned him to his fate, fastened myself to the cask by means of the lashings which secured it to the counter, and precipitated myself with it into the sea, without another moment's hesitation.

" The result was precisely what I had hoped it might be. As it is myself who now tell you this tale — as you see that I did escape — and as you are already in possession of the mode in which this escape was effected, and must therefore anticipate all that I have farther to say — I will bring my story quickly to conclusion. It might have been an hour, or thereabout, after my quitting the smack, when, having descended to a vast distance beneath me, it made three or four wild gyrations in rapid succession, and, bearing my loved brother with it, plunged headlong, at once and forever, into the chaos of foam below. The barrel to which I was attached sunk very little farther than half the distance between the bottom of the gulf and the spot at which I leaped overboard, before a great change took place in the character of the whirlpool. The slope of the sides of the vast funnel became momently less and less steep. The gyrations of the whirl grew, gradually, less and less violent. By degrees, the froth and the rainbow disappeared, and the bottom of the gulf seemed slowly to uprise. The sky was clear, the winds had gone down, and the full moon was setting radiantly in the west, when I found myself on the surface of the ocean, in full view of the shores of Lofoden, and above the spot where the pool of the Moskoe-ström had been. It was the hour of the slack — but the sea still heaved in mountainous waves from the effects of the hurricane. I was borne violently into the channel of the Ström, and in a few minutes was hurried down the coast into the "grounds" of the fishermen. A boat picked me up — exhausted from fatigue —

and (now that the danger was removed) speech-
less from the memory of its horror. Those who
drew me on board were my old mates and daily
companions — but they knew me no more than
they would have known a traveller from the
spirit-land. My hair which had been raven-
black the day before, was as white as you see it
now. They say too that the whole expression of
my countenance had changed. I told them my
story — they did not believe it. I now tell it
to you — and I can scarcely expect you to put
more faith in it than did the merry fishermen
of Lofoden."

# The Pit and the Pendulum

Impia tortorum longos hic turba furores
Sanguinis innocui, non satiata, aluit.
Sospite nunc patria, fracto nunc funeris
antro, Mors ubi dira fuit vita salusque
patent.

—Quatrain composed for the
gates of a market to be erected
upon the site of the Jacobin Club
House at Paris. [1]

I was sick — sick unto death with that
long agony; and when they at length unbound
me, and I was permitted to sit, I felt that my
senses were leaving me. The sentence — the
only for a brief period; for presently I heard
no more. Yet, for a while, I saw; but with

[1] Latin. "Here comes the impious clammer of
the torturers, insatiate, fed long its rage for inno-
cent blood. Now happy is the land, destroyed the pit
of horror, and where grim death stalked, life and
health are revealed."

dread sentence of death — was the last of distinct accentuation which reached my ears. After that, the sound of the inquisitorial voices seemed merged in one dreamy indeterminate hum. It conveyed to my soul the idea of revolution, perhaps from its association in fancy with the burr of a mill wheel. This only for a brief period; for presently I heard no more. Yet, for a while, I saw; but with how terrible an exaggeration! I saw the lips of the black-robed judges. They appeared to me white — whiter than the sheet upon which I trace these words — and thin even to grotesqueness; thin with the intensity of their expression of firmness — of immoveable resolution — of stern contempt of human torture. I saw that the decrees of what to me was Fate, were still issuing from those lips. I saw them writhe with a deadly locution. I saw them fashion the syllables of my name; and I shuddered because no sound succeeded. I saw, too, for a few moments of delirious horror, the soft and nearly imperceptible waving of the sable drap-

eries which enwrapped the walls of the apartment. And then my vision fell upon the seven
tall candles upon the table. At first they wore
the aspect of charity, and seemed white and
slender angels who would save me; but then,
all at once, there came a most deadly nausea
over my spirit, and I felt every fibre in my
frame thrill as if I had touched the wire of a
galvanic battery, while the angel forms became
meaningless spectres, with heads of flame, and
I saw that from them there would be no help.
And then there stole into my fancy, like a
rich musical note, the thought of what sweet rest
there must be in the grave. The thought came
gently and stealthily, and it seemed long before
it attained full appreciation; but just as my
spirit came at length properly to feel and enter-
tain it, the figures of the judges vanished, as
if magically, from before me; the tall candles
sank into nothingness; their flames went out
utterly; the blackness of darkness supervened;
all sensations appeared swallowed up in a mad-
rushing descent as of the soul into Hades. Then

silence, and stillness, night were the universe.

I had swooned; but still will not say that all of consciousness was lost. What of it there remained I will not attempt to define, or even to describe; yet all was not lost. In the deepest slumber — no! In delirium — no! In a swoon — no! In death — no! even in the grave all is not lost. Else there is no immortality for man. Arousing from the most profound of slumbers, we break the gossamer web of some dream. Yet in a second afterward, (so frail may that web have been) we remember not that we have dreamed. In the return to life from the swoon there are two stages; first, that of the sense of mental or spiritual; secondly, that of the sense of physical, existence. It seems probable that if, upon reaching the second stage, we could recall the impressions of the first, we should find these impressions eloquent in memories of the gulf beyond. And that gulf is — what? How at least shall we distinguish its shadows from those of the tomb?

But if the impressions of what I have termed the first stage, are not, at will, recalled, yet, after long interval, do they not come unbidden, while we marvel whence they come? He who has never swooned, is not he who finds strange palaces and wildly familiar faces in coals that glow; is not he who beholds floating in mid-air the sad visions that the many may not view; is not he who ponders over the perfume of some novel flower — is not he whose brain grows bewildered with the meaning of some musical cadence which has never before arrested his attention.

Amid frequent and thoughtful endeavors to remember; amid earnest struggles to regather some token of the state of seeming nothingness into which my soul had lapsed, there have been moments when I have dreamed of success; there have been brief, very brief periods when I have conjured up remembrances which the lucid reason of a later epoch assures me could have had reference only to that condition of seeming unconsciousness. These shadows of memory tell, indistinctly, of tall figures that lifted and bore me in silence down — down — still down — till a hideous dizziness oppressed me at the mere idea of the interminableness of the descent. They tell also of a vague horror at my heart, on account of that heart's unnatural stillness. Then comes a sense of sudden motionlessness throughout all things; as if those who bore me (a ghastly train!) had outrun, in their descent, the limits of the limitless, and paused from the wearisomeness of their toil. After this I call to mind flatness and dampness; and then all is madness — the madness of a memory which busies itself among forbidden things.

Very suddenly there came back to my soul motion and sound — the tumultuous motion of the heart, and, in my ears, the sound of its beating. Then a pause in which all is blank. Then again sound, and motion, and touch — a tingling sensation pervading my frame. Then the mere consciousness of existence, without thought — a condition which lasted long. Then, very suddenly, thought, and shudder-

69

ing terror, and earnest endeavor to comprehend
my true state. Then a strong desire to lapse
into insensibility. Then a rushing revival
of soul and a successful effort to move. And
now a full memory of the trial, of the judges,
of the sable draperies, of the sentence, of the
sickness, of the swoon. Then entire forgetful-
ness of all that followed; of all that a later
day and much earnestness of endeavor have
enabled me vaguely to recall.

So far, I had not opened my eyes. I
felt that I lay upon my back, unbound. I
reached out my hand, and it fell heavily upon
something damp and hard. There I suffered it
to remain for many minutes, while I strove to
imagine where and what I could be. I longed,
yet dared not to employ my vision. I dreaded
the first glance at objects around me. It was
not that I feared to look upon things horrible,
but that I grew aghast lest there should be
nothing to see. At length, with a wild desper-
ation at heart, I quickly unclosed my eyes.
My worst thoughts, then, were confirmed. The

blackness of eternal night encompassed me. I struggled for breath. The intensity of the darkness seemed to oppress and stifle me. The atmosphere was intolerably close. I still lay quietly, and made effort to exercise my reason. I brought to mind the inquisitorial proceedings, and attempted from that point to deduce my real condition. The sentence had passed; and it appeared to me that a very long interval of time had since elapsed. Yet not for a moment did I suppose myself actually dead. Such a supposition, notwithstanding what we read in fiction, is altogether inconsistent with real existence; — but where and in what state was I? The condemned to death, I knew, perished usually at the autos-da-fe, and one of these had been held on the very night of the day of my trial. Had I been remanded to my dungeon, to await the next sacrifice, which would not take place for many months? This I at once saw could not be. Victims had been in immediate demand. Moreover, my dungeon, as well as all the condemned cells at Toledo, had stone floors, and light was not altogether excluded.

A fearful idea now suddenly drove the blood in torrents upon my heart, and for a brief period, I once more relapsed into insensibility. Upon recovering, I at once started to my feet, trembling convulsively in every fibre. I thrust my arms wildly above and around me in all directions. I felt nothing; yet dreaded to move a step, lest I should be impeded by the walls of a tomb. Perspiration burst from every pore, and stood in cold big beads upon my forehead. The agony of suspense grew at length intolerable, and I cautiously moved forward, with my arms extended, and my eyes straining from their sockets, in the hope of catching some faint ray of light. I proceeded for many paces; but still all was blackness and vacancy. I breathed more freely. It seemed evident that mine was not, at least, the most hideous of fates.

And now, as I still continued to step cautiously onward, there came thronging upon my recollection a thousand vague rumors of the horrors of Toledo. Of the dungeons there had been strange things narrated — fables I had always deemed them — but yet strange, and too ghastly to repeat, save in a whisper. Was I left to perish of starvation in this subterranean world of darkness; or what fate, perhaps even more fearful, awaited me? That the result would be death, and a death of more than customary bitterness, I knew too well the character of my judges to doubt. The mode and the hour were all that occupied or distracted me.

My outstretched hands at length encountered some solid obstruction. It was a wall, seemingly of stone masonry — very smooth, slimy, and cold. I followed it up; stepping with all the careful distrust with which certain antique narratives had inspired me. This process, however, afforded me no means of ascertaining the dimensions of my dungeon; as I might make its circuit, and return to the point

73

whence I set out, without being aware of the fact; so perfectly uniform seemed the wall. I therefore sought the knife which had been in my pocket, when led into the inquisitorial chamber; but it was gone; my clothes had been exchanged for a wrapper of coarse serge. I had thought of forcing the blade in some minute crevice of the masonry, so as to identify my point of departure. The difficulty, nevertheless, was but trivial; although, in the disorder of my fancy, it seemed at first insuperable. I tore a part of the hem from the robe and placed the fragment at full length, and at right angles to the wall. In groping my way around the prison, I could not fail to encounter this rag upon completing the circuit. So, at least I thought; but I had not counted upon the extent of the dungeon, or upon my own weakness. The ground was moist and slippery. I staggered onward for some time, when I stumbled and fell. My excessive fatigue induced me to remain prostrate; and sleep soon overtook me as I lay.

Upon awaking, and stretching forth an arm, I found beside me a loaf and a pitcher with water. I was too much exhausted to reflect upon this circumstance, but ate and drank with avidity. Shortly afterward, I resumed my tour around the prison, and with much toil came at last upon the fragment of the serge. Up to the period when I fell I had counted fifty-two paces, and upon resuming my walk, I had counted forty-eight more; — when I arrived at the rag. There were in all, then, a hundred paces; and, admitting two paces to the yard, I presumed the dungeon to be fifty yards in circuit. I had met, however, with many angles in the wall, and thus I could form no guess at the shape of the vault; for vault I could not help supposing it to be.

I had little object — certainly no hope — in these researches; but a vague curiosity prompted me to continue them. Quitting the wall, I resolved to cross the area of the enclosure. At first I proceeded with extreme caution, for the floor, although seemingly of solid material, was treacherous with slime. At length, however, I took courage, and did not hesitate to step firmly; endeavoring to cross in as direct a line as possible. I had advanced some ten or twelve paces in this manner, when the remnant of the torn hem of my robe became entangled between my legs. I stepped on it, and fell violently on my face.

In the confusion attending my fall, I did not immediately apprehend a somewhat startling circumstance, which yet, in a few seconds afterward, and while I still lay prostrate, arrested my attention. It was this — my chin rested upon the floor of the prison, but my lips and the upper portion of my head, although seemingly at a less elevation than the chin, touched nothing. At the same time my forehead seemed bathed in a clammy vapor, and the peculiar smell of decayed fungus arose to my nostrils. I put forward my arm, and shuddered to find that I had fallen at the very brink of a circular pit, whose extent, of course,

I had no means of ascertaining at the moment. Groping about the masonry just below the margin, I succeeded in dislodging a small fragment, and let it fall into the abyss. For many seconds I hearkened to its reverberations as it dashed against the sides of the chasm in its descent; at length there was a sullen plunge into water, succeeded by loud echoes. At the same moment there came a sound resembling the quick opening, and as rapid closing of a door overhead, while a faint gleam of light flashed suddenly through the gloom, and as suddenly faded away.

I saw clearly the doom which had been prepared for me, and congratulated myself upon the timely accident by which I had escaped. Another step before my fall, and the world had seen me no more. And the death just avoided, was of that very character which I had regarded as fabulous and frivolous in the tales respecting the Inquisition. To the victims of its tyranny, there was the choice of death with its direst physical agonies, or death with its most

77

hideous moral horrors. I had been reserved for the latter. By long suffering my nerves had been unstrung, until I trembled at the sound of my own voice, and had become in every respect a fitting subject for the species of torture which awaited me.

Shaking in every limb, I groped my way back to the wall; resolving there to perish rather than risk the terrors of the wells, of which my imagination now pictured many in various positions about the dungeon. In other conditions of mind I might have had courage to end my misery at once by a plunge into one of these abysses; but now I was the veriest of cowards. Neither could I forget what I had read of these pits — that the sudden extinction of life formed no part of their most horrible plan.

Agitation of spirit kept me awake for many long hours; but at length I again slumbered. Upon arousing, I found by my side, as before, a loaf and a pitcher of water. A burning thirst consumed me, and I emptied the vessel

at a draught. It must have been drugged; for
scarcely had I drunk, before I became irresist-
ibly drowsy. A deep sleep fell upon me — a
sleep like that of death. How long it lasted of
course, I know not; but when, once again, I
unclosed my eyes, the objects around me were
visible. By a wild sulphurous lustre, the
origin of which I could not at first determine,
I was enabled to see the extent and aspect of
the prison.

In its size I had been greatly mistaken.
The whole circuit of its walls did not exceed
twenty-five yards. For some minutes this fact
occasioned me a world of vain trouble; vain
indeed — for what could be of less importance,
under the terrible circumstances which environed
me, then the mere dimensions of my dungeon?
But my soul took a wild interest in trifles,
and I busied myself in endeavors to account
for the error I had committed in my measure-
ment. The truth at length flashed upon me. In
my first attempt at exploration I had counted
fifty-two paces, up to the period when I fell; I

must then have been within a pace or two of the fragment of serge ; in fact , I had nearly performed the circuit of the vault . I then slept, and upon awaking , I must have returned upon my steps — thus supposing the circuit nearly double what it actually was . My confusion of mind prevented me from observing that I began my tour with the wall to the left, and ended it with the wall to the right .

I had been deceived , too, in respect to the shape of the enclosure . In feeling my way I had found many angles , and thus deduced an idea of great irregularity ; so potent is the effect of total darkness upon one arousing from leth- argy or sleep ! The angles were simply those of a few slight depressions, or niches, at odd inter- vals . The general shape of the prison was square . What I had taken for masonry seemed now to be iron, or some other metal , in huge plates , whose sutures or joints occasioned the depression . The entire surface of this metallic enclosure was rudely daubed in all the hideous and repulsive devices to which the charnel superstition of the monks has given rise. The figures of fiends in aspects of menace, with skeleton forms, and other more really fearful images, overspread and disfigured the walls. I observed that the outlines of these monstrosities were sufficiently distinct, but that the colors seemed faded and blurred, as if from the effects of a damp atmosphere. I now noticed the floor, too, which was of stone. In the centre yawned the circular pit from whose jaws I had escaped; but it was the only one in the dungeon.

All this I saw indistinctly and by much effort: for my personal condition had been greatly changed during slumber. I now lay upon my back, and at full length, on a species of low framework of wood. To this I was securely bound by a long strap resembling a surcingle. It passed in many convolutions about my limbs and body, leaving at liberty only my head, and my left arm to such extent that I could, by dint of much exertion, supply myself with food from an earthen dish which lay by my side on the floor. I saw, to my horror, that the pitcher had been removed. I say to my horror; for I was consumed with intolerable thirst. This thirst it appeared to be the design of my persecutors to stimulate, for the food in the dish was meat pungently seasoned.

Looking upward, I surveyed the ceiling of my prison. It was some thirty or forty feet overhead, and constructed much as the side walls. In one of its panels a very singular figure riveted my whole attention. It was the painted figure of Time as he is commonly represented, save that, in lieu of a scythe, he held what, at a casual glance, I supposed to be the pictured image of a huge pendulum such as we see on antique clocks. There was something, however, in the appearance of this machine which caused me to regard it more attentively. While I gazed directly upward at it (for its position was immediately over my own) I fancied that I saw it in motion. In an instant afterward the fancy was confirmed. Its sweep was brief, and of course slow. I watched it for some minutes, somewhat in fear, but more in wonder. Wearied at length with observing its dull movement, I turned my eyes upon the other objects in the cell.

A slight noise attracted my notice, and, looking to the floor. I saw several enormous rats traversing it. They had issued from the well, which lay just within view to my right. Even then, while I gazed, they came up in troops, hurriedly, with ravenous eyes, allured by the scent of the meat. From this it required much effort and attention to scare them away.

It might have been half an hour, perhaps even an hour, (for I could take but imperfect note of time) before I again cast my eyes upward. What I then saw confounded and amazed me. The sweep of the pendulum had increased in extent by nearly a yard. As a natural consequence, its velocity was also much greater. But what mainly disturbed me was the idea

83

that had perceptibly descended. I now observed
— with what horror it is needless to say — that
its nether extremity was formed of a crescent of
glittering steel, about a foot in length from
horn to horn; the horns upward, and the under
edge evidently as keen as that of a razor. Like
a razor also, it seemed massy and heavy,
tapering from the edge into a solid and broad
structure above. It was appended to a weighty
rod of brass, and the whole hissed as it swung
through the air.

I could no longer doubt the doom prepared
for me by monkish ingenuity in torture. My
cognizance of the pit had become known to the
inquisitorial agents — the pit, whose horrors
had been destined for so bold a recusant as
myself — the pit, typical of hell, and regarded
by rumor as the Ultima Thule of all their pun-
ishments. The plunge into this pit I had
avoided by the merest of accidents, I knew that
surprise, or entrapment into torment, formed
an important portion of all the grotesquerie of
these dungeon deaths. Having failed to fall, it

was no part of the demon plan to hurl me into the abyss; and thus (there being no alternative) a different and a milder destruction awaited me. Milder! I half smiled in my agony as I thought of such application of such a term.

What boots it to tell of the long, long hours of horror more than mortal, during which I counted the rushing vibrations of the steel! Inch by inch — line by line — with a descent only appreciable at intervals that seemed ages — down and still down it came! Days passed — it might have been that many days passed — ere it swept so closely over me as to fan me with its acrid breath. The odor of the sharp steel forced itself into my nostrils. I prayed — I wearied heaven with my prayer for its more speedy descent. I grew frantically mad, and struggled to force myself upward against the sweep of the fearful scimitar. And then I fell suddenly calm, and lay smiling at the glittering death, as a child at some rare bauble.

There was another interval of utter insensibility; it was brief; for, upon again lapsing into life there had been no perceptible descent in the pendulum. But it might have been long; for I knew there were demons who took note of my swoon, and who could have arrested the vibration at pleasure. Upon my recovery, too, I felt very — oh, inexpressibly sick and weak, as if through long inanition. Even amid the agonies of that period, the human nature craved food. With painful effort I outstretched my left arm as far as my bonds permitted, and took possession of the small remnant which had been spared me by the rats. As I put a portion of it within my lips, there rushed to my mind a half formed thought of joy — of hope. Yet what business had I with hope? It was, as I say, a half formed thought — man has many such which are never completed. I felt that it was of joy — of hope; but felt also that it had perished in its formation. In vain I struggled to perfect — to regain it. Long suffering had nearly annihilated all my ordinary powers of mind. I was an imbecile — an idiot.

The vibration of the pendulum was at right angles to my length. I saw that the crescent was designed to cross the region of the heart. It would fray the serge of my robe — it would return and repeat its operations — again — and again. Notwithstanding terrifically wide sweep (some thirty feet or more) and the hissing vigor of its descent, sufficient to sunder these very walls of iron, still the fraying of my robe would be all that, for several minutes, it would accomplish. And at this thought I paused. I dared not go farther than this reflection. I dwelt upon it with a pertinacity of attention — as if, in so dwelling, I could arrest here the descent of the steel. I forced myself to ponder upon the sound of the crescent as it should pass across the garment — upon the peculiar thrilling sensation which the friction of cloth produces on the nerves. I pondered upon all this frivolity until my teeth were on edge.

Down — steadily down it crept. I took a frenzied pleasure in contrasting its downward with its lateral velocity. To the right — to the left — far and wide — with the shriek of a damned spirit; to my heart with the stealthy pace of the tiger! I alternately laughed and howled as the one or the other idea grew predominant.

Down — certainly, relentlessly down! It vibrated within three inches of my bosom! I struggled violently, furiously, to free my left arm. This was free only from the elbow to the hand. I could reach the latter, from the platter beside me, to my mouth, with great effort, but no farther. Could I have broken the fastenings above the elbow, I would have seized and attempted to arrest the pendulum. I might as well have attempted to arrest an avalanche!

Down — still unceasingly — still inevitably down! I gasped and struggled at each vibration. I shrunk convulsively at its every sweep. My eyes followed its outward or upward

whirls with the eagerness of the most unmean-
ing despair; they closed themselves spasmodic-
ally at the descent, although death would have
been a relief, oh, how unspeakable! Still I
quivered in every nerve to think how slight a
sinking of the machinery would precipitate that
keen, glistening axe upon my bosom. It was
hope that prompted the nerve to quiver — the
frame to shrink. It was hope — the hope that
triumphs on the rack — that whispers to the
death-condemned even in the dungeons of the
Inquisition.

I saw that some ten or twelve vibrations
would bring the steel in actual contact with my
robe, and with this observation there suddenly
came over my spirit all the keen, collected
calmness of despair. For the first time during
many hours — or perhaps days — I thought.
It now occurred to me that the bandage, or surcingle, which enveloped me, was unique. I
was tied by no separate cord. The first stroke
of the razorlike crescent athwart any portion of
the band, would so detach it that it might be

unwound from my person by means of my left hand. But how fearful, in that case, the proximity of the steel! The result of the slightest struggle how deadly! Was it likely, moreover, that the minions of the torturer had not foreseen and provided for this possibility! Was it probable that the bandage crossed my bosom in the track of the pendulum? Dreading to find my faint, and, as it seemed, in last hope frustrated, I so far elevated my head as to obtain a distinct view of my breast. The surcingle enveloped my limbs and body close in all directions — save in the path of the destroying crescent.

Scarcely had I dropped my head back into its original position, when there flashed upon my mind what I cannot better describe than as the unformed half of that idea of deliverance to which I have previously alluded, and of which a moiety only floated indeterminately through my brain when I raised food to my burning lips. The whole thought was now present — feeble, scarcely sane, scarcely definite, — but still entire. I proceeded at once, with the nervous energy of despair, to attempt its execution.

For many hours the immediate vicinity of the low framework upon which I lay, had been literally swarming with rats. They were wild, bold, ravenous; their red eyes glaring upon me as if they waited but for motionlessness on my part to make me their prey. "To what food," I thought, "have they been accustomed in the well?"

They had devoured, in spite of all my efforts to prevent them, all but a small remnant of the contents of the dish. I had fallen into an habitual see-saw, or wave of the hand about the platter: and, at length, the unconscious uniformity of the movement deprived it of effect. In their voracity the vermin frequently fastened their sharp fangs in my fingers. With the particles of the oily and spicy viand which now remained, I thoroughly rubbed the bandage wherever I could reach it; then, raising my hand from the floor, I lay breathlessly still.

At first the ravenous animals were startled and terrified at the change — at the cessation of movement. They shrank alarmedly back; many sought the well. But this was only for a moment. I had not counted in vain upon their voracity. Observing that I remained without motion, one or two of the boldest leaped upon the framework, and smelt at the surcingle. This seemed the signal for a general rush. Forth from the well they hurried in fresh troops. They clung to the wood — they overran it, and leaped in hundreds upon my person. The measured movement of the pendulum disturbed them not at all. Avoiding its strokes they busied themselves with the anointed bandage. They pressed — they swarmed upon me in ever accumulating heaps. They writhed upon my throat; their cold lips sought my own; I was half stifled by their thronging pressure; disgust, for which the world has no name, swelled my bosom, and chilled, with a heavy clamminess, my heart. Yet one minute, and I felt that the struggle would be over. Plainly I perceived the loosening of the bandage. I knew that in more than one place it must be already severed. With a more than human resolution I lay still.

Nor had I erred in my calculations — nor had I endured in vain. I at length felt that I was free. The surcingle hung in ribands from my body. But the stroke of the pendulum already pressed upon my bosom. It had divided the serge of the robe. It had cut through the linen beneath. Twice again it swung, and a sharp sense of pain shot through every nerve. But the moment of escape had arrived. At a wave of my hand my deliverers hurried tumultuously away. With a steady movement — cautious, sidelong, shrinking, and slow — I slid from the embrace of the bandage and beyond the reach of the scimitar. For the moment, at least, I was free.

Free! — and in the grasp of the Inquisition! I had scarcely stepped from my wooden bed of horror upon the stone floor of the prison, when the motion of the hellish machine ceased and I beheld it drawn up, by some invisible force, through the ceiling. This was a lesson

93

which I took desperately to heart . My every motion was undoubtedly watched . Free ! — I had but escaped death in one form of agony, to be delivered unto worse than death in some other . With that thought I rolled my eyes nervously around on the barriers of iron that hemmed me in . Something unusual — some change which , at first, I could not appreciate distinctly — it was obvious, had taken place in the apartment . For many minutes of a dreamy and trembling abstraction , I busied myself in vain , unconnected conjecture . During this period, I became aware, for the first time , of the origin of the sulphurous light which illumined the cell . It proceeded from a fissure, about half an inch in width , extending entirely around the prison at the base of the walls, which thus appeared, and were , completely separated from the floor . I endeavored , but of course in vain , to look through the aperture .

As I arose from the attempt, the mystery of the alteration in the chamber broke at once upon my understanding . I have observed that , although the outlines of the figures upon the walls were sufficiently distinct, yet the colors seemed blurred and indefinite. These colors had now assumed, and were momentarily assuming, a startling and most intense brilliancy, that gave to the spectral and fiendish portraitures an aspect that might have thrilled even firmer nerves than my own. Demon eyes, of a wild and ghastly vivacity, glared upon me in a thousand directions, where none had been visible before, and gleamed with the lurid lustre of a fire that I could not force my imagination to regard as unreal.

Unreal! — Even while I breathed there came to my nostrils the breath of the vapour of heated iron! A suffocating odour pervaded the prison! A deeper glow settled each moment in the eyes that glared at my agonies! A richer tint of crimson diffused itself over the pictured horrors of blood. I panted! I gasped for breath! There could be no doubt of the design of my tormentors — oh! most unrelenting! oh! most demoniac of men! I shrank from the glowing metal to the centre of the cell. Amid the thought of the fiery destruction that impended, the idea of the coolness of the well came over my soul like balm. I rushed to its deadly brink. I threw my straining vision below. The glare from the enkindled roof illumined its inmost recesses. Yet, for a wild moment, did my spirit refuse to comprehend the meaning of what I saw. At length it forced — it wrestled its way into my soul — it burned itself in upon my shuddering reason. — Oh! for a voice to speak! — oh! horror! — oh! any horror but this! With a shriek, I rushed from the margin, and buried my face in my hands — weeping bitterly.

The heat rapidly increased, and once again I looked up, shuddering as with a fit of the ague. There had been a second change in the cell — and now the change was obviously in the form. As before, it was in vain that I, at first, endeavoured to appreciate or understand what was taking place. But not long was I left in doubt. The Inquisitorial vengeance had been hurried by my two-fold escape, and there was to be no more dallying with the King of Terrors. The room had been square. I saw that two of its iron angles were now acute — two, consequently, obtuse. The fearful difference quickly increased with a low rumbling or moaning sound. In an instant the apartment had shifted its form into that of a lozenge. But the alteration stopped not here — I neither hoped nor desired it to stop. I could have clasped the red walls to my bosom as a garment of eternal peace. " Death ," I said , " any death but that of the pit ! " Fool ! might I have not known that into the pit it was the object of the burning iron to urge me ? Could I resist its glow ? or, if even that, could I withstand its pressure ? And now, flatter and flatter grew the lozenge , with a rapidity that left me no time for contemplation. Its centre, and of course, its greatest width, came just over the yawning gulf. I shrank back — but the closing walls pressed me resistlessly onward. At length for my seared and writhing body there was no longer an inch of foothold on the firm floor of the prison. I struggled no more , but the agony of my soul found vent in one loud, long, and final scream of despair. I felt that I tottered upon the brink — I averted my eyes —

There was a discordant hum of human voices! There was a loud blast as of many trumpets! There was a harsh grating as of a thousand thunders! The fiery walls rushed back! An outstretched arm caught my own as I fell, fainting, into the abyss. It was that of General Lasalle. The French army had entered Toledo. The Inquisition was in the hands of its enemies.

# The Masque of the Red Death

The "Red Death" had long devastated the country. No pestilence had ever been so fatal, or so hideous. Blood was its Avatar and its seal — the redness and the horror of blood. There were sharp pains, and sudden dizziness, and then profuse bleeding at the pores, with dissolution. The scarlet stains upon the body and especially upon the face of the victim, were the pest ban which shut him out from the aid and from the sympathy of his fellow-men. And the whole seizure, progress and termination of the disease, were the incidents of half an hour.

But the Prince Prospero was happy and dauntless and sagacious. When his dominions were half depopulated, he summoned to his presence a thousand hale and light-hearted friends from among the knights and dames of his court, and with these retired to the deep seclusion of one of his castellated abbeys. This was an extensive and magnificent structure, the creation of the prince's own eccentric yet august taste. A strong

and lofty wall girdled it in. This wall had
gates of iron. The courtiers, having entered,
brought furnaces and massy hammers and
welded the bolts. They resolved to leave means
neither of ingress nor egress to the sudden
impulses of despair or of frenzy from within.
The abbey was amply provisioned. With such
precautions the courtiers might bid defiance to
contagion. The external world could take care of
itself. In the meantime it was folly to grieve, or
to think. The prince had provided all the appli-
ances of pleasure. There were buffoons, there
were improvisatori, there were ballet-dancers,
there were musicians, there was Beauty, there was
wine. All these and security were within. Without was the "Red Death".

It was towards the close of the fifth or
sixth month of his seclusion, and while the
pestilence raged most furiously abroad, that the
Prince Prospero entertained his thousand friends
at a masked ball of the most unusual magnificence.

101

It was a voluptuous scene, that masquerade. But first let me tell of the rooms in which it was held. These were seven — an imperial suite. In many palaces, however, such suites form a long and straight vista, while the folding doors slide back nearly to the walls on either hand, so that the view of the whole extent is scarcely impeded. Here the case was very different, as might have been expected from the duke's love of the bizarre. The apartments were so irregularly disposed that the vision embraced but little more than one at a time. There was a sharp turn at every twenty or thirty yards, and at each turn a novel effect. To the right and left, in the middle of each wall, a tall and narrow Gothic window looked out upon a closed corridor which pursued the windings of the suite. These windows were of stained glass whose colour varied in accordance with the prevailing hue of the decorations of the chamber into which it opened. That at the eastern extremity was hung, for example in blue — and vividly blue were its windows. The second chamber was purple in its ornaments and tapestries, and here the panes were purple. The third was green throughout, and so were the casements. The fourth was furnished and lighted with orange — the fifth with white — the sixth with violet. The seventh apartment was closely shrouded in black velvet tapestries that hung all over the ceiling and down the walls, falling in heavy folds upon a carpet of the same material and hue. But in this chamber only, the colour of the windows failed to correspond with the decorations. The panes here were scarlet — a deep blood colour. Now in no one of the seven apartments was there any lamp or candelabrum, amid the profusion of golden ornaments that lay scattered to and fro or depended from the roof. There was no light of any kind emanating from lamp or candle within the suite of chambers. But in the corridors that followed the suite, there stood, opposite to each window, a heavy tripod, bearing a brazier of fire, that projected its rays through the tinted glass and so glaringly illumined the room. And thus were produced a multitude of gaudy and fantastic appearances. But in the western or black chamber the effect of the fire-light that streamed upon the dark hangings through the blood-tinted panes, was ghastly in the extreme, and produced so wild a look upon the countenances of those who entered, that there were few of the company bold enough to set foot within its precincts at all.

It was in this apartment, also, that there stood against the western wall, a gigantic clock of ebony. Its pendulum swung to and fro with a dull, heavy, monotonous clang; and when the minute-hand made the circuit of the face, and the hour was to be stricken, there came from the brazen lungs of the clock a sound which was clear and loud and deep and exceedingly musical, but of so peculiar a note and emphasis that, at each lapse of an hour, the musicians of the orchestra were constrained to pause, momentarily, in their performance, to harken to the sound; and thus the waltzers perforce ceased their evolutions; and there was a brief disconcert of the whole gay company; and, while the chimes of the clock yet rang, it was observed that the giddiest grew pale, and the more aged and sedate passed their hands over their brows as if in confused revery or meditation. But when the echoes had fully ceased, a light laughter at once pervaded the assembly; the musicians looked at each other and smiled as if at their own nervousness and folly, and made whispering vows, each to the other, that the next chiming of the clock should produce in them no similar emotion; and then, after the lapse of sixty minutes, (which embrace three thousand and six hundred seconds of the Time that flies), there came yet another chiming of the clock, and then were the same disconcert and tremulousness and meditation as before.

But, in spite of these things, it was a gay and magnificent revel. The tastes of the duke were peculiar. He had a fine eye for colours and effects. He disregarded the decora of mere fashion. His plans were bold and fiery, and his conceptions glowed with barbaric lustre. There are some who would have thought him mad. His followers felt that he was not. It was necessary to hear and see and touch him to be sure that he was not.

He had directed, in great part, the movable embellishments of the seven chambers, upon occasion of this great fête; and it was his own guiding taste which had given character to the masqueraders. Be sure they were grotesque. There were much glare and glitter and piquancy and phantasm — much of what has been since seen in "Hernani". There were arabesque figures with unsuited limbs and appointments. There were delirious fancies such as the madman fashions. There were much of the beautiful, much of the wanton, much of the bizarre, something of the terrible, and not a little of that which might have excited disgust. To and fro in the seven chambers there stalked, in fact, a multitude of dreams. And these — the dreams — writhed in and about taking hue from the rooms, and causing the wild music of the orchestra to seem as the echo of their steps. And, anon, there strikes the ebony clock which stands in the hall of the velvet. And then, for a moment, all is still, and all is silent save the voice of the clock. The dreams are stiff-frozen as they stand. But the echoes of the chime die away — they have endured but an instant — and a light, half-subdued laughter floats after them as they depart. And now again the music swells, and the dreams live, and writhe to and fro more merrily than ever, taking hue from the many tinted windows through which stream the rays from the tripods. But to the chamber which lies most westwardly of the seven, there are now none of the maskers who venture; for the night is waning away; and there flows a ruddier light through the blood-coloured panes; and the blackness of the sable drapery appals; and to him whose foot falls upon the sable carpet, there comes from the near clock of ebony a muffled peal more solemnly emphatic than any which reaches their ears who indulged in the more remote gaieties of the other apartments.

But these other apartments were densely crowded, and in them beat feverishly the heart of life. And the revel went whirlingly on, until at length there commenced the sounding of midnight upon the clock. And then the music ceased, as I have told; and the evolutions of the waltzers were quieted; and there was an uneasy cessation of all things as before. But now there were twelve strokes to be sounded by the bell of the clock; and thus it happened, perhaps, that more of thought crept, with more of time, into the meditations of the thoughtful among those who revelled. And thus too, it happened, perhaps, that before the last echoes of the last chime had utterly sunk into silence, there were many individuals in the crowd who had found leisure to become aware of the presence of a masked figure which had arrested the attention of no single individual before. And the rumour of this new presence having spread itself whisperingly around, there arose at length from the whole company a buzz, or murmur, expressive of disapprobation and surprise — then, finally, of terror, of horror, and of disgust.

In an assembly of phantasms such as I have painted, it may well be supposed that no ordinary appearance could have excited such sensation. In truth the masquerade licence of the night was nearly unlimited; but the figure

in question had out-Heroded Herod, and gone
beyond the bounds of even the prince's indefinite decorum. There are chords in the hearts of
the most reckless which cannot be touched without emotion. Even with the utterly lost, to
whom life and death are equally jests, there are
matters of which no jest can be made. The
whole company, indeed, seemed now deeply to
feel that in the costume and bearing of the
stranger neither wit nor propriety existed. The
figure was tall and gaunt, and shrouded from
head to foot in the habiliments of the grave.
The mask which concealed the visage was made so
nearly to resemble the countenance of a stif-
fened corpse that the closest scrutiny must have
had difficulty in detecting the cheat. And yet
all this might have been endured, if not
approved, by the mad revellers around. But
the mummer had gone so far as to assume the
type of the Red Death. His vesture was dabbled
in blood — and his broad brow, with all the
features of the face, was besprinkled with the
scarlet horror.

109

When the eyes of the Prince Prospero fell upon this spectral image (which, with a slow and solemn movement, as if more fully to sustain its role, stalked to and fro among the waltzers) he was seen to be convulsed, in the first moment with a strong shudder either of terror or distaste; but, in the next, his brow reddened with rage.

"Who dares;" — he demanded hoarsely of the courtiers who stood near him — " who dares insult us with this blasphemous mockery? Seize him and unmask him — that we may know whom we have to hang, at sunrise, from the battlements!"

It was in the eastern or blue chamber in which stood the Prince Prospero as he uttered these words. They rang throughout the seven rooms loudly and clearly, for the prince was a bold and robust man, and the music had become hushed at the waving of his hand.

It was in the blue room where stood the prince, with a group of pale courtiers by his side. At first, as he spoke, there was a slight rushing movement of this group in the direction of the intruder, who at the moment was also near at hand, and now, with deliberate and stately step, made closer approach to the speaker. But from a certain nameless awe with which the mad assumptions of the mummer had inspired the whole party, there were found none who put forth hand to seize him; so that, unimpeded, he passed within a yard of the prince's person; and, while the vast assembly, as if with one impulse, shrank from the centres of the rooms to the walls, he made his way uninterruptedly, but with the same solemn and measured step which had distinguished him from the first, through the blue chamber to the purple — through the purple to the green — through the green to the orange — through this again to the white — and even thence to the violet, ere a decided movement had been made to arrest him. It was then, however, that the Prince Prospero, maddening with rage and the shame of his own momentary cowardice, rushed hurriedly through the six chambers, while none followed him on

111

account of a deadly terror that had seized upon all. He bore aloft a drawn dagger, and had approached, in rapid impetuosity, to within three or four feet of the retreating figure, when the latter, having attained the extremity of the velvet apartment, turned suddenly and confronted his pursuer. There was a sharp cry — and the dagger dropped gleaming upon the sable carpet, upon which, instantly afterwards, fell prostrate in death the Prince Prospero. Then, summoning the wild courage of despair, a throng of the revellers at once threw themselves into the black apartment, and, seizing the mummer, whose tall figure stood erect and motionless within the shadow of the ebony clock, gasped in unutterable horror at finding the grave cerements and corpse-like mask, which they handled with so violent a rudeness, untenanted by any tangible form.

And now was acknowledged the presence of the Red Death. He had come like a thief in the night. And one by one dropped the revellers in the blood-bedewed halls of their revel, and died

each in the despairing posture of his fall. And
the life of the ebony clock went out with that of
the last of the gay. And the flames of the tripods expired. And Darkness and Decay and the
Red Death held illimitable dominion over all.

# Lenore.

Ah, broken is the golden bowl !  the spirit flown forever !
Let the bell toll ! __ a saintly soul floats on the Stygian river .
And, Guy de Vere , hast thou no tear ? __ weep now or never more !
See ! on yon drear and rigid bier low lies thy love, Lenore !
Come !  let the burial rite be read __  the funeral song be sung ! __
An anthem for the queenliest dead that ever died so young —
A dirge for her, the doubly dead in that she died so young .

"Wretches ! ye loved her for her wealth and hated her for her pride ;
And when she fell in feeble health, ye blessed her—that she died !
How shall the ritual, then, be read ? __ the requiem how be sung

By you — by yours, the evil eye, — by yours,
the slanderous tongue
That did to death the innocence that died, and
died so young?"

Peccavimus ; but rave not thus ! and let a
Sabbath song
Go up to God so solemnly the dead may feel no
wrong !
The sweet Lenore hath "gone before ," with Hope,
that flew beside ,
Leaving thee wild for the dear child that should
have been thy bride —
For her , the fair and débonnaire , that now so
lowly lies ,
The life upon her yellow hair but not within
her eyes —
The life still there , upon her hair — the death
upon her eyes .

"Avaunt ! to-night my heart is light . No
dirge will I upraise ,
But waft the angel on her flight with a paean of
old days !
Let no bell toll ! — lest her sweet soul, amid
its hallowed mirth ,

Should catch the note, as it doth float up from the
damned Earth.
To friends above, from fiends below, the
indignant ghost is riven —
From Hell unto a high estate far up within the
Heaven —
From grief and groan to a golden throne beside
the King of Heaven."

*The Raven* first appeared in print in the *New York Evening Mirror* on January 29, 1845 and was an instant sensation, making Edgar Allan Poe an overnight celebrity. The popularity of a poem that initially only earned Poe a meager $15 (equivalent to $491 in 2023) left the author to lament, "I have made no money. I am as poor now as ever I was in my life—except in hope, which is by no means bankable."

Initially Poe conceived of an owl and even a parrot as the ethereal visitor in his poem, but ultimately opted for the appropriate mystique of the raven, which, in mythology- like the owl- is a psychopomp or spirit that escorts the soul to the afterlife. Poe had seen death all his life, but no death affected him as profoundly as that of his wife, Virginia, who had brought him so much warmth and frivolity that was a welcome distraction. His grief was so consuming that it seemed necessary to give it an identity- a presence that loomed over him day and night, unyielding forever more.

The following pages spotlight restorations of original materials that were handwritten by Poe, including the only existing manuscript of the poem, which was requested by Poe's friend Eli Bowen as a gift for Dr. Samuel Adams Whitaker and is currently part of the Gimbel Collection at the Free Library of Philadelphia.

The following materials have been tilted horizontally for larger character size:

117

Dear Shea,

Lest I should have made some mistake in the hurry I transcribe the whole alteration.

Instead of the whole stanza commencing "Wondering at the stillness broken &c — substitute this

Startled at the stillness broken by reply so aptly spoken,
"Doubtless", said I, "what it utters is its only stock and store
Caught from some unhappy master whom unmerciful Disaster
Followed fast and followed faster till his songs one burden bore
Till the dirges of his Hope the melancholy burden bore,
          'Nevermore — ah, nevermore!'"

At the close of the stanza _preceding_ this, instead of
"Quoth the raven Nevermore", substitute "Then the
bird said "Nevermore".

Truly yours
Poe

# The Raven.

Once, upon a midnight dreary, while I pondered, weak and weary,
Over many a quaint and curious volume of forgotten lore —
While I nodded, nearly napping, suddenly there came a tapping,
As of some one gently rapping, rapping at my chamber door.
" 'Tis some visiter," I muttered, "tapping at my chamber door —
        Only this and nothing more."

Ah, distinctly I remember it was in the bleak December,
And each separate dying ember wrought its ghost upon the floor.
Eagerly I wished the morrow ;— vainly I had sought to borrow
From my books surcease of sorrow — sorrow for the lost Lenore —
For the rare and radiant maiden whom the angels name Lenore —
        Nameless here for evermore.

And the silken, sad, uncertain rustling of each purple curtain
Thrilled me, filled me with fantastic terrors never felt before;
So that now, to still the beating of my heart, I stood repeating
" 'Tis some visiter entreating entrance at my chamber door —
Some late visiter entreating entrance at my chamber door; —
                              This it is and nothing more."

Presently my soul grew stronger. Hesitating, then, no longer,
"Sir", said I, or Madam, truly your forgiveness I implore;
But the fact is I was napping, and so gently you came rapping,
And so faintly you came tapping, tapping at my chamber door
That I scarce was sure I heard you" — here I opened wide the door; —
                              Darkness there and nothing more.

Deep into that darkness peering, long I stood there, wondering, fearing,
Doubting, dreaming dreams no mortal ever dared to dream before;
But the silence was unbroken, and the stillness gave no token,
And the only word there spoken was the whispered word, "Lenore?"
This I whispered, and an echo murmured back the word "Lenore!"—
             Merely this and nothing more.

Back into the chamber turning, all my soul within me burning,
Soon again I heard a tapping somewhat louder than before.
"Surely", said I, "surely that is something at my window lattice;
Let me see, then, what thereat is. and this mystery explore;—
Let my heart be still a moment ┐and this mystery explore;—
             'Tis the wind and nothing more."

Open here I flung the shutter, when, with many a flirt and flutter,
In there stepped a stately Raven of the saintly days of yore.
Not the least obeisance made he; not a minute stopped or stayed he;
But, with mien of lord or lady, perched above my chamber door —
Perched upon a bust of Pallas just above my chamber door —
Perched and sat and nothing more.

Then this ebony bird beguiling my sad fancy into smiling,
By the grave and stern decorum of the countenance it wore,
"Though thy crest be shorn and shaven, thou", I said "art sure no craven
Ghastly, grim and ancient Raven, wandering from the Nightly shore —
Tell me what thy lordly name is on the Night's Plutonian shore!"
Quoth the Raven, "Nevermore."

Much I marvelled this ungainly fowl to hear discourse so plainly,
Though its answer little meaning — little relevancy bore ;
For we cannot help agreeing that no living human being
Ever yet was blessed with seeing bird above his chamber door —
Bird or beast upon the sculptured bust above his chamber door,
                              With such name as "Nevermore".

But the Raven, sitting lonely on that placid bust, spoke only
That one word, as if his soul in that one word he did outpour.
Nothing farther then he uttered ; not a feather then he fluttered —
Till I scarcely more than muttered — "Other friends have flown before —
On the morrow he will leave me, as my Hopes have flown before."
                              Then the Bird said "Nevermore."

Startled at the stillness broken by reply so aptly spoken,
"Doubtless", said I, "what it utters is its only stock and store,
Caught from some unhappy master whom unmerciful Disaster
Followed fast and followed faster, till his songs one burden bore —
Till the dirges of his Hope that melancholy burden bore
                    Of 'Never — nevermore.' "

But the Raven still beguiling all my sad soul into smiling,
Straight I wheeled a cushioned seat in front of bird and bust and door;
Then, upon the velvet sinking, I betook myself to linking
Fancy unto fancy, thinking what this ominous bird of yore —
What this grim, ungainly, ghastly, gaunt and ominous bird of yore
                    Meant in croaking "Nevermore".

This I sat engaged in guessing, but no syllable expressing
To the fowl whose fiery eyes now burned into my bosom's core;
This and more I sat divining, with my head at ease reclining
On the cushion's velvet lining that the lamp-light gloated o'er,
But whose velvet, violet lining with the lamp-light gloating o'er
_She_ shall press, ah, nevermore!

Then, methought, the air grew denser, perfumed from an unseen censer
Swung by Seraphim whose foot-falls tinkled on the tufted floor.
"Wretch", I cried, "thy God hath lent thee — by these angels he hath sent thee
Respite — respite and nepenthe from thy memories of Lenore!
Quaff, oh quaff this kind nepenthe and forget this lost Lenore!"
Quoth the Raven "Nevermore."

"Prophet!" said I, "thing of evil! — prophet still, if bird or devil! —
Whether Tempter sent or whether tempest tossed thee here ashore,
Desolate yet all undaunted, on this desert land enchanted —
On this home by Horror haunted — tell me truly, I implore —
Is there — is there balm in Gilead? — tell me — tell me, I implore!"
            Quoth the Raven "Nevermore".

"Prophet!" said I, "thing of evil! — prophet still, if bird or devil!
By that Heaven that bends above us — by that God we both adore —
Tell this soul with sorrow laden if, within the distant Aidenn,
It shall clasp a sainted maiden whom the angels name Lenore —
Clasp a rare and radiant maiden whom the angels name Lenore."
            Quoth the Raven "Nevermore".

Be that word our sign of parting, bird or fiend!" I shrieked, upstarting —
"Get thee back into the tempest and the Night's Plutonian shore!
Leave no black plume as a token of that lie thy soul hath spoken!
Leave my loneliness unbroken! — quit the bust above my door!
Take thy beak from out my heart and take thy form from off my door!
            Quoth the Raven "Nevermore".

And the Raven, never flitting, still is sitting — still is sitting
On the pallid bust of Pallas just above my chamber door;
And his eyes have all the seeming of a demon's that is dreaming,
And the lamp-light o'er him streaming throws his shadow on the floor;
And my soul from out that shadow that lies floating on the floor
            Shall be lifted —— nevermore.

Inscribed to Dr. S. A. Whittaker
of Phœnixville.

Edgar A. Poe.

# The City in the Sea.

Lo! Death has reared himself a throne
In a strange city lying alone
Far down within the dim West
Where the good and the bad and the worst
and the best
Have gone to their eternal rest.
There shrines and palaces and towers
(Time-eaten towers and tremble not !)
Resemble nothing that is ours .
Around, by lifting winds forgot ,
Resignedly beneath the sky
The melancholy waters lie .
No rays from the holy Heaven come down
On the long night-time of that town ;
But light from out the lurid sea
Streams up the turrets silently —
Gleams up the pinnacles far and free —
Up domes — up spires — up kingly halls —
Up fanes — up Babylon-like walls —
Up shadowy long-forgotten bowers
Of sculptured ivy and stone flowers —
Up many and many a marvellous shrine

Whose wreathed friezes intertwine
The viol, the violet, and the vine.
Resignedly beneath the sky
The melancholy waters lie.
So blend the turrets and shadows there
That all seem pendulous in air,
While from a proud tower in the town
Death looks gigantically down.
There open fanes and gaping graves
Yawn level with the luminous waves;
But not the riches there that lie
In each idol's diamond eye —
Not the gaily-jewelled dead
Tempt the waters from their bed;
For no ripples curl, alas!
Along that wilderness of glass —
No swellings tell that winds may be
Upon some far-off happier sea —
No heavings hint that winds have been
On seas less hideously serene.
But lo, a stir is in the air!
The wave — there is a movement there!
As if the towers had thrust aside,
In slightly sinking, the dull tide —
As if their tops had feebly given

A void within the filmy Heaven.
The waves have now a redder glow —
The hours are breathing faint and low —
And when, amid no earthly moans,
Down, down that town shall settle hence,
Hell, rising from a thousand thrones,
Shall do it reverence.

# Eulalie

I dwelt alone
    In a world of moan,
And my soul was a stagnant tide
Till the fair and gentle Eulalie became my blushing bride —
Till the yellow-haired young Eulalie became my smiling bride.

    Ah, less, less bright
        The stars of the night
Than the eyes of the radiant girl,
        And never a flake
            That the vapor can make
With the moon-tints of purple and pearl,
Can vie with the modest Eulalie's most unregarded curl —
Can compare with the bright-eyed Eulalie's most humble and careless
                                                        } curl.

        Now Doubt — now Pain
            Come never again,
For her soul gives me sigh for sigh,
            And all day long
                Shines bright and strong
Astarté within the sky,
While ever to her dear Eulalie upturns her matron eye —
While ever to her young Eulalie upturns her violet eye.

# <u>Virginia's Valentine Poem for Poe</u>

John Sartain's eulogy in the Introduction to this book was as an invaluable character study of Poe as is the following poem gifted to Poe by wife Virginia for Valentine's Day. Popular in this era of early America were acrostic poems, in which each line begins with the letters that spell out the recipient's name. No doubt penned with Poe's own haunting quill, this is the only known poem by Virginia as she had only a rudimentary education and total lack of interest in poetry altogether (even poetry by Poe did little to excite her).

Virginia's poem makes mention of her 'weakened lungs', alluding to tuberculosis that she had contracted just four years prior. Tuberculosis or "The Red Death" was a dogged part of Poe's life and it has been speculated that he may have been a carrier without ever showing symptoms of his own. Poe's first exposure to TB was at the tender of age of 3, when his mother, Eliza, succumbed to the disease. Both Poe's step-mother, Frances, and his step-brother, Henry, died of the disease (although the cause of death for the latter remains questionable). Jane Stanard died of TB (the woman Poe called "Helen"), who was the mother of his closest class-mate, Robert. Poe's love interest, Frances Sargent Osgood, also contracted the terminal illness. As for

poor Virginia, she died less than one year after
penning the following poem:

Ever with thee I wish to roam—
Dearest my life is thine.
Give me a cottage for my home
And a rich old cypress vine,
Removed from the world with its sin and care
And the tattling of many tongues.
Love alone shall guide us when we are there—
Love shall heal my weakened lungs;
And Oh, the tranquil hours we'll spend,
Never wishing that others may see!
Perfect ease we'll enjoy, without thinking to lend
Ourselves to the world and its glee.—
Ever peaceful and blissful we'll be.
      Saturday February 14. 1846.

# Annabel Lee.
## By Edgar A. Poe.

It was many and many a year ago,
  In a kingdom by the sea,
That a maiden there lived whom you may know
  By the name of Annabel Lee; —
And this maiden she lived with no other thought
  Than to love and be loved by me.

She was a child and I was a child,
  In this kingdom by the sea,
But we loved with a love that was more than love —
  I and my Annabel Lee —
With a love that the winged seraphs of Heaven
  Coveted her and me.

And this was the reason that, long ago,
  In this kingdom by the sea,
A wind blew out of a cloud by night
  Chilling my Annabel Lee;
So that her high-born kinsmen came
  And bore her away from me,
To shut her up in a sepulcre
  In this kingdom by the sea.

The angels, not half so happy in Heaven,
        Went envying her and me :—
Yes! that was the reason (as all men know,
        In this kingdom by the sea)
That the wind came out of the cloud, chilling
        And killing my Annabel Lee.


But our love it was stronger by far than the love
        Of those who were older than we —
        Of many far wiser than we —
And neither the angels in Heaven above
        Nor the demons down under the sea
Can ever dissever my soul from the soul
        Of the beautiful Annabel Lee :—


For the moon never beams without bringing me dreams
        Of the beautiful Annabel Lee;
And the stars never rise but I see the bright eyes
        Of the beautiful Annabel Lee;
And so, all the night-tide, I lie down by the side
Of my darling, my darling, my life and my bride
        In her sepulchre there by the sea —
        In her tomb by the side of the sea.

139

# Memorable Quotes of E. A. Poe

"Man's real life is happy, chiefly because he is ever expecting that it soon will be so."

"Words have no power to impress the mind without the exquisite horror of their reality."

"To observe attentively is to remember distinctly."

"All that we see or seem, is but a dream within a dream."

"I would define, in brief, the poetry of words as the rhythmical creation of Beauty."

"I became insane, with long intervals of horrible sanity."

"I have great faith in fools; my friends call it self-confidence."

"Those who dream by day are cognizant of many things which escape those who dream only by night."

"I was never really insane except upon occasions when my heart was touched."

"There is no exquisite beauty... without some strangeness in the proportion."

"Believe nothing you hear, and only one half that you see."

"Tell me every terrible thing you ever did, and let me love you anyway."

"Our existence is but a brief crack of light between two eternities of darkness."

"There are some secrets that do not permit themselves to be told."

"Years of love had been forgot, in the hatred of a minute."

"Art is to look at, not to criticize."

"Every poem should remind the reader that they are going to die."

"It is a happiness to wonder- it is a happiness to dream."

"To die laughing must be the most glorious of all deaths!"

* 9 7 9 8 8 9 5 8 9 8 8 2 6 *